Grandad

Written by

Rachel Elliot

Illustrated by

Katie Pamment

little bee

D0543297

My Grandad lives
in a gypsy caravan.

Mum says he lives
in another world.

When Grandad wears out his old boots,
he fills them with soft red earth
and grows flowers in them.
The steps outside the
caravan are covered in
old boots and big flowers.

Grandad calls it
Flower Power.

When Grandad was
young he had long hair,
just like mine.

But now, he hasn't
got much at all.

Grandad says...

the wind blew it away...

...like a dandelion clock.

After breakfast we play cowboys.
We use the washing line as a lasso.
Grandad lassoes Mrs Brown.

Grandad's old bike rattles
when it goes down the hill to the beach.
Our teeth rattle too!

"My poor old bones!"
says Grandad.

We watch the waves splashing
and feed the seagulls.
I have two ice creams.
Grandad has three.

"Life's for living!" says Grandad.

Grandad can play the guitar.
He teaches me the old songs.
We sit on the beach and sing them together

— VERY LOUD.

He calls it our music festival.

When we get home, we decorate the caravan
with the shells we have collected.

I stick some onto the ceiling.

They look like
moon rocks!

When Grandad cooks tea, the air is full of spices.
Curry is his favourite.

"The hotter the better," says Grandad.

We eat our tea on
the caravan steps
and watch
for ships.

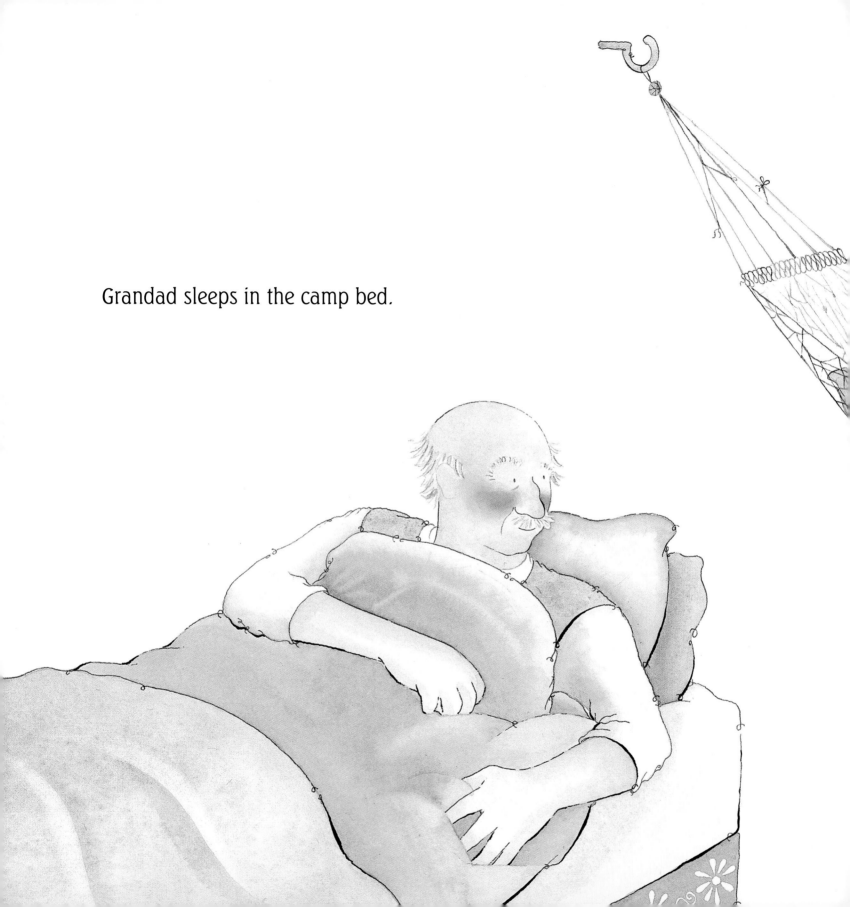

Grandad sleeps in the camp bed.

I get the hammock.

When I climb in, the whole caravan creaks.

"Safe as houses,"
says Grandad.

My Grandad is the best storyteller in the world.

And tonight...

...I might just creep down
to the bottom of the garden,
up the caravan steps...

And listen to Grandad's stories
until I fall asleep.

For Ken, with all my love.
R.E.

To Margaret Appa, the best teacher in the world,
and with happy memories of my own grandparents.
K.P.

This edition published 2009 by Little Bee
an imprint of Meadowside Children's Books

First published in 2005
by Meadowside Children's Books
185 Fleet Street
London EC4A 2HS

Text © Rachel Elliot 2005
Illustrations © Katie Pamment 2005
The rights of Rachel Elliot to be
identified as the author
and Katie Pamment to be identified
as the illustrator of this work have been
asserted by them in accordance with
the Copyright, Designs and
Patents Act, 1988

A CIP catalogue record for this book
is available from the British Library
10 9 8 7 6 5 4 3 2 1
Printed in Malaysia